SHAKTI

THE STORY OF A HOMELESS WOMAN IN INDIA

PAM MANDY

This book has been published with all efforts taken to make the material error-free after the consent of the author. However, the author and the publisher do not assume and hereby disclaim any liability to any party for any loss, damage, or disruption caused by errors or omissions, whether such errors or omissions result from negligence, accident, or any other cause.

While every effort has been made to avoid any mistake or omission, this publication is being sold on the condition and understanding that neither the author nor the publishers or printers would be liable in any manner to any person by reason of any mistake or omission in this publication or for any action taken or omitted to be taken or advice rendered or accepted on the basis of this work. For any defect in printing or binding the publishers will be liable only to replace the defective copy by another copy of this work then available.

Disclaimer

While the author has strived to ensure the accuracy of the information, she makes no claims, warranties or representations about the completeness, reliability or accuracy of the information provided in this book. The interpretation of the data presented in this book is purely from the author's point of view and the author assumes no responsibility or liability from any individual or entity for any disputes legal or otherwise, that may arise on the content of this book. This book is for informational and educational purposes only.

Dedication

To my soulmate, Jay, whose constant love and support have enriched all walks of my life.

Acknowledgment

I would like to thank Mr. Avijit Karmakar, a freelance painter who specializes in portraiture and landscaping, for providing excellent illustrations for this book. He can be reached at 8272981758 or 81003 88451.

Contents

Contents

Foreword

My association with Pam started when both of us pursued our graduate studies in Cultural Anthropology, under the excellent mentorship of Dr. Sudarshan, a eminent Anthropologist at Madras University. Pam went to the United States to pursue her doctoral degree. Our friendship grew stronger over the years, strengthened by our common interests in women's issues, particularly those relating to gender, family, status and equality in India.

Shakti: *The Story of a Homeless Woman in India*, is an excellent fictional narrative which offers keen insights into the lives of homeless women living on the streets of Chennai, India. Written in a compelling manner, the story of Shakti brings to light the struggles and survival strategies of homeless women. Deprived of traditional male support in their lives due to death and abandonment, these homeless women are forced to look for alternate support systems. An emphasis is also placed on the role of traditional religious institutions such as major temples in Chennai which offer a sense of safe space as well as offering opportunities for earning a livelihood to the homeless women of Chennai. Larger issues such as migration and urban poverty, changing gender roles, the role of female centered networks are woven into the fabric of the narrative. This book is a must-read for any one who is interested in issues of gender and inequality within the complex social and cultural structure of the Indian subcontinent.

Dr. S. Sumathi

University of Madras

Preface

S hakti: *The Story of a Homeless Woman in India* is the outcome of a series of conversations with a homeless woman called Shakti and five of her friends who were living on the streets of Chennai, India. Having lived in Chennai for a few years during my young adulthood, I have crossed paths with homeless people countless times. However, I had never paid any significant attention to them. To me, these people did not seem to exist. Occasionally, a homeless woman or child would grab my attention by asking for food or money, and I always avoided them and turned away. Then, one day, I met a homeless woman called Shakti.

When I initially met her, I did not know Shakti was homeless. Contrary to my opinions at that time about homeless women, she was neatly dressed and had a pleasant personality. Shakti was exceptionally effective in the art of communicating, and she had a wealth of information to share.

Over time, Shakti told me about herself, her family, her friends, and her life before and after she became homeless. The more I learned about her, the more my impressions about homeless people changed.

Shakti permitted me to record our conversations, and soon, I had a wealth of data that provided important insights into the lives of homeless women living on the streets of Chennai. Shakti and her friends lived near a big temple in an urban locality in the city. I conducted and recorded open-ended interviews with five of her friends to corroborate her story.

My conversations with Shakti and her friends raised some important questions in my mind about her life and the lives of other homeless women. Who were these women? What kind of socio-economic backgrounds did they come from? Were they from previously male-dominated support systems? What kinds of alternative support systems have replaced them? I wanted to find out if these new support systems were dominated by women and what, if any, were the bonds between these women? Had the single mothers become less dependent on men? What were the economic activities of these homeless women? How did they support themselves and their children? How did women like Shakti view themselves? How did others view them? This book aims to find answers to some of these questions through the narration of Shakti's story.

The more I listened to the recorded conversations with Shakti and her friends, the more I was inspired to share my knowledge with others, especially those who held stereotypical views of the homeless as lazy or crazy. The courage and fortitude of the homeless women in the face of overt and covert discrimination made me realize there is more to them than meets the eye. I wish to present these strong women to my readers through the narration of Shakti's story. The names of people and places have been changed to protect their identities. Shakti is pronounced Sakti in some Tamil-speaking areas.

Chapter 1

A Starry Night

Slowly, a drop of water trickled down her cheek. Startled, she woke up and hastily brushed it away before anyone could notice it. Was it a tear rolling down her cheek in quiet desperation, or was rainwater pouring down from the skies above? Shakti had slept under the midnight stars a few hours earlier, not because she was camping or star-gazing at some exotic vacation resort, but because she was homeless. By now, the rain was beating down mercilessly on her. She quickly looked down to see her two children waking up to raindrops falling on them and quickly drenching their clothes. Her daughter, Ponni, who was eight, and her son, Kadir, who was three, were still drowsy from sleep, but they quickly followed their mother to the shelter of a large awning of a nearby grocery store. Other homeless people, still drowsy from sleep, soon followed them, making space for each other as everyone tried to stay dry. A couple of mangy dogs also followed them, wet and miserable, their tails between their legs. Men, women, and children soon huddled together. After all, it was not their first experience avoiding rain, and they knew exactly what to do.

The sound of heavy rainfall drowned the cries of babies whose sleep had been rudely disrupted by the rain, as well as the soothing voices of their mothers or older siblings who were trying to calm them down. The crowd waited in miserable silence for the rain to stop. Even the dogs had quieted down. There was nowhere else to go and nothing else to do. Shakti and her children tried to lie down on the bare floor of the crowded storefront and eventually fell into a slumber. It was still dark, and sunrise was still a few hours away. Soon, the surrounding open areas, which were dotted with the bodies of sleeping homeless people only moments ago, looked totally deserted.

Chapter 2

Sunshine and Laughter

Life was not always wet and miserable for Shakti. There was a time when her life was filled with warmth and sunshine, and she was very happy, when she was living with her parents and her younger sister Mohana in a small mud house with a thatched roof. This was their home in their village, which provided shelter from the elements. Both sisters thrived in the warmth of their parents' unconditional love. Shakti often fondly remembered playing with her sister for countless hours in the sunshine while their parents worked on the small piece of land next to their home, where they grew vegetables for their family.

Shakti adored her family, particularly her mother. The void that her mother's death had left in her heart was never filled, and dreams of her parents were a recurring theme in her life. *What a wonderful and loving mother she was,* Shakti thought often, and she sometimes reached out her arms as if she could feel secure in her mother's warm hug once more. Shakti remembered her mother's beautiful face looking down at her as she told her daughter why she had picked that particular name for her. Shakti, her mother had explained, was the embodiment of the cosmic female power revered as Durga, Parvati, and Kaali, among others, and was believed to vanquish mighty demons with her special powers. Just like these goddesses, Shakti's mother had said, her daughter was strong and could accomplish whatever task she set her mind to. Shakti smiled reminiscently as she remembered how she always thought of herself as independent and capable of dealing with any situation. Little did she know when she was growing up that all her strengths would be tested one day and that she had to muster all her inner strength just to survive.

Shakti and Mohana were thought to be the prettiest girls in their village. There was no shortage of male admirers; wherever they went, they drew much attention. Free social interactions between men and women were not encouraged in their community then, and the sisters were perfectly happy to be admired from afar until Raja came into their lives. He was the most handsome man Shakti had ever met. He was older than her by a few years and, in her eyes, incredibly charming. They soon fell deeply in love. It was the happiest time in her life as they spent long afternoons and evenings discussing their dreams and aspirations for a great future together.

Both sets of parents blessed the young couple, and life seemed perfect. Raja was full of excitement as he painted a picture of a glorious future for them. He told his beloved that the big city of Chennai presented them with multiple opportunities for bettering their future compared to their small village. Raja had been talking to his cousin Guna, who had left their village with his wife and two young children to move to Chennai a few months earlier. Guna had described in detail how big the metropolis was and how he and his wife could always find work. There were so many things to enjoy in the city; he had told Raja, focusing particularly on the super hit movies of some of the major actors in the Tamil film industry.

Raja's excitement soon won Shakti over, and they started planning to migrate to Chennai.

After all, Guna and his family were not the only ones who had left their village in search of a better life. Two of her aunts and their husbands had left for Chennai five years earlier. The fact that they never came back to visit the village was never discussed. Shakti ignored the small voice inside her that told her she would be leaving all that was familiar and dear to her by going away to the distant city. She would not be able to see her parents and Mohana, as well as her friends and relatives who had formed the fabric of her life in their village. The thought of losing Raja was unbearable, as he was determined to move to Chennai, with or without her. Eventually, their love for each other won, and the journey to Chennai was planned after the wedding.

The wedding day dawned with bright sunshine. The little mud house was decorated with colorful paints and fresh flowers. The sound of music filled the air as a rental stereo blared popular film songs. A few elderly women were busy cooking a feast. A goat was slaughtered for this special occasion, and most villagers were part of the festivities. Surrounded by their family and friends, the bride and groom looked resplendent in their new clothes. Shakti proudly wore the gold earrings and necklace that her parents had given her as a wedding gift. A bride who did not bring any gold jewelry was not shown much respect in their village. She knew how her mother had skimped and saved every rupee to buy the gold jewelry. It was the best day of her life.

After the wedding festivities, the newlyweds set a date for their departure to Chennai. When Shakti told her parents about their move to Chennai in search of better opportunities, there was a moment of silence. Her parents quickly hid their worry and concern about their daughter's leaving and encouraged the young couple by blessing them with happiness and prosperity. Mohana was fully supportive of her sister's decision. She had also found love and was excited about her upcoming marriage. Shakti assured her parents and Mohana that she and Raja would never forget them and that they would visit them frequently.

Soon, it was time to say goodbye. The sinking feeling in the pit of her stomach when she saw her parents' eyes filled with tears had to be suppressed. As she and Raja walked away to the bus station to begin their journey to Chennai, she couldn't help looking back again and again. She could not see their faces because of the tears that filled her eyes. As she turned the corner, Shakti looked back one last time, and the image of her parents and Mohana waving goodbye with tearful eyes would remain with her forever.

...

Chapter 3

Chasing a Rainbow

The bus journey to Chennai was uneventful. For most of the journey, Shakti slept with her head on her husband's shoulder, lulled by the swaying of the bus. In a half-awake state of mind, her thoughts wandered to dwell on all the good things in store for them in the city—a nice home, good jobs that provided enough money for a comfortable lifestyle. There would be no dearth of food or nice clothes. Eventually, their family would grow to include children. Visions of her parents playing with their grandchildren filled her mind. As the bus approached Chennai, Shakti was full of dreams for a bright and happy future.

She woke up with a start when the bus stopped. Chennai was huge! That was Shakti's first impression when she got off the bus at the city bus station. There were people everywhere! She stood wide-eyed and tried to take in the hustle and bustle of a busy metropolis. Car drivers honked impatiently, demanding that pedestrians get out of their way. Crowds of people got in and out of buses and autos. Bicyclists added more chaos to this congested traffic scene. Darting in between were hundreds of people walking in a hurry to reach their destinations. Along the periphery of the bus station, Shakti noticed some men, women, and children sitting or sleeping. Some families were engaged in cooking and chatting with each other. She wondered who these people were. Little did she know that one day she would join them as a part of the city's homeless population.

Life seemed exciting. Shakti clung to her husband's arm as he scanned the people around him, looking for a familiar face. They were waiting for his cousin, Guna, with whom they would stay for a few days until they found their place to live. Suddenly, they heard a loud voice calling their names and turned to see their cousin smiling and waving at them. He seemed happy to see them and took them to his house. His wife, Mullai, had cooked a hot meal of rice and lentil soup, and Raja and Shakti were thankful that they had a place to sleep that night.

The first few weeks were a blur of activity. Raja's cousin lived with his family in a makeshift home near the bus station. Guna and Mullai welcomed the new immigrants into their small house and provided food and other necessities. After the initial excitement had died down, Shakti started noticing other things around her. She observed that Guna and his family wore torn and used clothes. Food was also scarce, as they did not have the small piece of land like her parents had, back in their village, where they could grow fruits and vegetables to meet the needs of their families.

Guna and his wife went looking for work every day, leaving their younger daughter, who was three years old, with her older sister, who was barely twelve. *This would never have happened in our village,* thought Shakti. The elders in the joint family watched over the young children when their parents went to work. But many migrants had to leave their extended family behind in their quest for a better future. Shakti's heart melted when she thought of the twelve-year-old girl who had to grow up too soon to become a caregiver for her younger sibling. She knew that was the fate of many children of poor migrants who could not afford to hire caregivers, and who had no extended family in the city.

After a few days, Raja went out every day with his cousin in search of a job. He found odd jobs for the day, either as a day laborer at construction sites or as an agricultural worker. Most days, he brought home a couple of hundred rupees which was barely enough to meet their daily needs. Raja worked hard to provide for his young bride. Many evenings, he would come home tired and with a nasty headache. Shakti always kept some hot food for him and would massage his aching head until he fell asleep. There were days when Raja could not find any work and had to return home empty-handed. Those days were hard. Either they ate leftovers or Guna and his wife helped them out by offering them food.

Raja and Shakti wanted to move out on their own. Even though Guna and his wife showed great hospitality, they felt it was time to start their independent life in Chennai. Before they could find a place of their own, a series of events, over which they had no control, unfolded and changed the course of their life forever.

A deep depression in the Bay of Bengal turned the streets of Chennai into flowing rivers. A continuous torrent of rain poured down, flooding roads and alleys. The rainfall was so heavy that it washed away the little hut that was home to Shakti and Raja as well as Guna's family. It seemed as though the whole family became homeless overnight. *What are we going to do?* Shakti wondered desperately. She and her husband were stuck in a new place that had suddenly turned into a hostile environment. When Guna decided to return to their village, Shakti and Raja felt lonelier than ever. For a moment, they, too, considered returning to the village—at least they would have their parents' support and a roof over their heads. But this thought lasted only for a moment as they could visualize the mocking smiles and hurtful comments of people in their community who would mock their failure in not accomplishing their goal of going to the city to make a better life for themselves. *We would rather die here in Chennai rather than return to our village in shame*, Shakti thought, and Raja agreed.

Since the piece of land on which their hut had stood was filled with water, the young couple had to decide their next steps soon. With their meager belongings wrapped in plastic bags and old clothes, they wondered where they would spend the next night. Guna and his family had already left for the village, and Raja and Shakti did not know many people in Chennai. Raja remembered an elderly aunt who had visited them in their village a few months before they had moved to Chennai. When Raja asked her where she lived, the aunt told them that she lived near a big temple near the bus station. She had told them that the temple provided a sense of safety for her, as she was alone. Also, food was relatively easy to get because of the small jobs that were available near the temple.

Shakti and Raja decided that they would spend the night near the temple and stay there for a few days until they figured out what they were going to do. They thought that once they had enough money saved to rent a small house, they would leave the temple proximity. Shakti and Raja believed that this predicament was only temporary. Little did they know that there were more unfortunate circumstances to come.

Shakti and Raja departed on their journey to the temple. It took them a few hours to reach the temple. Soon, they could catch a glimpse of the temple in the distance. Standing tall and majestic was the temple tower, which immediately gave Shakti a sense of security. As they got closer to the temple, they could see small groups of mostly women and children or single elderly women sitting in the open space in front of the temple. Since it was already getting dark, some were cooking on small fires while others were talking with each other, and some were sleeping on mattresses made from pieces of old clothing, their belongings stacked close by.

It was not very difficult to locate the elderly aunt, Poovai. When she saw Shakti and Raja, Poovai was initially surprised, but after listening to their story, she understood their difficult situation. She quickly cleaned the space around her living area and welcomed the newcomers. Fortunately, she had some money with her, and with that, she bought groceries and cooked a simple meal of rice and lentils. After dinner, all three of them sat talking late into the night about what had happened. Soon, a makeshift bed was made for Raja and Shakti with old clothes and bed sheets. At first, it was very difficult for Shakti to settle down and sleep in an open area with no roof over her head, but she had no choice. Staring at the star-studded sky above, she suddenly sat up, and the magnitude of her situation hit her hard for the first time. Raja was lying down next to her with his eyes closed. Shakti was not sure if he was really asleep or if he was trying to shut out their reality from his mind. She slowly lay back and closed her eyes, but it was a long time before she could fall asleep. Thus ended Shakti and Raja's first night as part of the city's homeless population.

· · ·

Chapter 4

Life on the Streets

Poovai helped the young couple during their first few days as homeless people. According to Poovai, the temple provided a haven for people like them. She told Raja how a stranger had informed her about this temple when she had become homeless after her husband died. Like her nephew and his new wife, Poovai and her husband had sought the big city many years ago in quest of new opportunities. Like many migrants, they found odd jobs, barely making enough money to survive. Poovai wanted to return to their village, but her husband refused. He told his wife he could not face the humiliation of being considered a failure by his friends and family back home. Soon, both developed health problems, which made it hard for them to work, and they could not afford to pay their rent. After her husband's death, Poovai had nowhere to go and ended up near the temple.

After hearing Raja's aunt talk about the temple and the advantages of living nearby, Shakti and Raja decided to stay there for a few days and call it their home. They had already noticed that they were not the only homeless people living near the temple's vicinity. A quick count revealed to Shakti that at least twenty-five to forty people seemed to be living there. Most of them were women, and many had young children. *What happened to their husbands?* she wondered. She was about to discover exactly what happened a few months later.

The first few days around the temple were a blur of activity, and adjusting to a life in public view was extremely difficult for the young couple. This meant certain things that people think of as private activities, such as bathing, changing clothes, and sleeping, had to be done in full view of everyone. Shakti found it incredibly embarrassing to bathe and change in the open. Again, Poovai came to her rescue. Shakti quickly learned that the cover of darkness provided her with much-needed privacy. She started waking up in the early morning hours to bathe and wash her clothes at the water pump near the temple. Other women provided privacy to the bathing woman by standing in a group around her to ward off prying eyes. Even though there were fights and arguments among the women about who was at the pump first, they helped each other in times of need.

The most challenging and embarrassing times were when Raja wanted to be intimate with her. There was no privacy, and usually, they had to wait for the cover of darkness. Even then, Shakti was conscious of the other homeless people sleeping nearby. The unspoken code of honor was to pretend that nothing was happening. Shakti knew that single women like her friend Kanaka had male partners who visited them after dark. These nocturnal visits provided fuel for gossip the next day. When one of the women became pregnant, there was much speculation about who the father might be. Shakti and her friends worried about the possibility of their young children witnessing some inappropriate activity, but they could not do anything about it.

Shakti soon realized that there were no cupboards or lockers to safeguard their meager belongings, mostly worn-out clothes and aluminum pots and pans. Any expensive items, such as gold jewelry that some women had inherited from their mothers, were sold or pawned off. Shakti too had to sell her gold earrings and necklace when they had no money for food in the early days when they were living with Guna.

In the initial days near the temple, Shakti and Raja had identified a specific place in the open area that they called 'home'. They cooked and slept in the same place every day, and others never encroached. Women would leave their belongings in their spots when they went to work, and those who stayed back kept a close watch.

Babysitting was also a shared arrangement. At any given time, all small infants who had no older siblings to watch them while their parents worked were taken care of by women who were not working that particular day. Older women offered to babysit in exchange for food, noticed Shakti. Women first provided food to their children as well as the ones in their charge and ate only if anything was left over after feeding them.

Shakti would often wait for the occasional free food that came her way. This was a unique feature associated with the temple. Devotees offered food to their favorite deities, and this food was sometimes distributed to the poor people living outside the temple. Word spread around quickly that food would be distributed on a particular day, and most of the homeless ensured they were in line.

Even though Shakti and her homeless friends identified the temple vicinity as their home, they had never entered the temple. Once, she and a friend were turned away by the temple watchman when they wanted to go inside the temple. There was a big argument, and they had to walk away before the police were called to stop the ensuing brawl. Shakti never made an attempt to enter the temple again as she had never felt so humiliated.

Slowly, the weeks turned into months, and before Shakti and Raja realized it, a year had passed. They had formed strong bonds of friendship within their homeless community and felt a sense of belonging. Each day was still a struggle for survival, and both Shakti and Raja constantly thought of ways to get out of their predicament.

Chapter 5

Work Today; Eat Tonight

The hustle and bustle of the temple made it a busy place throughout the day. Surrounding the temple were rows of small stores catering to the demands of devotees and tourists. These stores sold assorted items such as fresh flower garlands, fruits and other worship materials, idols of different deities, small toys, and trinkets.

Survival near the temple meant being alert and aware of the surroundings. This included being on constant lookout for any job opportunities that might come their way. Since most of the work available to the homeless women near the temple fell under the daily wage category, it was available to those who asked for it first. Shakti was a quick learner. She had already noticed that the row of stores provided much-needed opportunities for work. Fresh flowers played a very important role in the worship of deities in the temple, and as such, there was a great demand for fresh flower garlands. The store owners catered to this demand by purchasing loose flowers from the city's flower market every morning and having them made into garlands. Shakti noticed that the store owners hired homeless women who lived nearby to make these garlands because they provided cheap labor. Since these jobs were offered to whoever approached the store owner first, there was always a competition of who would catch the eye of the store owner who was looking to hire a garland maker. Shakti was often first in line and usually found enough work every day for a few hours making fresh flower garlands. This work was usually open during morning hours only as the supply of fresh flowers would be exhausted quickly. The earnings from garland making were not enough even to buy food for a family for that day.

Since Shakti and most of her friends were paid less than 25 cents/20 rupees a day for making fresh flower garlands, they had to look for other small jobs. She soon observed that there was an opportunity to make some money by guarding devotees' and tourists' footwear when they visited the temple. This was because wearing footwear was prohibited inside the temple. *In order to get people's attention, one has to have a loud voice,* thought Shakti with amusement. The women sat in front of the temple and shouted to devotees and tourists, persuading them to leave their footwear in their care. A small fee was paid to the homeless women in charge of guarding footwear, and more footwear meant a few extra rupees, which meant one more meal.

Some homeless women who lived near the temple, preferring the stability of a monthly income to the uncertainty of daily earnings, introduced Shakti to another line of work. The houses that lined the four streets surrounding the temple offered some homeless women an opportunity to work as domestic help. Their services included cleaning, laundry, and washing dirty pots and pans. In return, they were paid around 10–15 dollars (about 600 to 700 rupees) a month. Offering domestic help in the neighborhood houses had some advantages—sometimes they were given leftover food and discarded clothes. Some kind employers gave money to homeless women as a loan without charging any interest when they had a health or other emergency. Shakti was thankful that her employer had given her some money when she had to visit the doctor for her back pain.

While some days offered promise of income, Shakti dreaded certain days when there would be no work, which meant no money for food. Those were the hardest days. She had seen her homeless friends, especially those with young children, take recourse to begging. They would go to each house in the neighborhood asking for money or leftover food. Shakti had vowed to herself that she would never do that; she did not like how the residents treated these women. They used harsh words toward the women standing on their doorstep asking for food. Shakti's heart melted when she thought of her friend Karuppai and women like her, who were either too old or too sick even to walk a few steps. Such women just sat near the temple entrance and tried to catch the attention of passers-by by calling out to them loudly for alms. Shakti never resorted to this method of making an extra buck. She knew that the older women would often compete with each other to show who was afflicted with more dreadful disease or disability—real or imaginary. The reason behind this was to attract the attention of tourists and devotees, who gave them a few rupees, pitying their condition.

International tourists were given special attention because they were so overwhelmed at seeing these homeless women begging for food. They were usually appalled to see so much poverty, pain, and suffering right in front of their eyes and hence would give more money.

While Shakti tried to earn money every day in one way or another, Raja tried to make ends meet by finding daily wage work outside the temple. His new friends, who also lived near the temple, took him along and showed him where they worked as daily laborers. Soon, Raja found work there, and he could find work on most days. Shakti never really knew what kind of work Raja did and how much money he made. Raja also did not tell his wife the nature of his work—he just gave her a couple of hundred rupees on the days he found work.

When Shakti and Raja both found work, they would buy groceries from the nearby store. She cooked his favorite food and would buy some delicacies from the nearby restaurant. Those were happy days, and if there were a few extra rupees, Raja would take Shakti to see her favorite film. Shakti loved to watch her favorite heroes on the big screens, especially those who made promises to better the lives of poor people. She sat spellbound with tears rolling down her cheeks as she watched emotionally charged scenes. In those few hours, they would forget their real-life struggles and escape into the world of make-believe.

Chapter 6

Entries and Exits

At first, Shakti thought that she had missed her monthly period because of stress. After all, she had become homeless and had to deal with the daily struggles of living on the streets. Stress was no stranger to Shakti, and she had all the following reasons and more to feel stressed—finding work every day, cooking and sleeping in the open area, lack of privacy for personal care, and no place to call home, among many others.

Soon, Shakti realized that it was more than stress that was messing with her monthly cycles. The possibility that she might be pregnant occurred, only to be promptly dismissed. Shakti was not ready to have a baby. She worriedly told Poovai, who was the only relative she had in Chennai. Poovai, with all her wisdom and years of experience, told Shakti that she thought a baby was on the way. A quick visit to the nearby doctor's clinic confirmed that this was indeed true. Shakti was going to be a mother.

The realization that she was going to bring a new life into this world brought tears to her eyes. Tears of happiness that she was having a baby and tears of sadness that she was going to give birth to a baby with no home. Having children had always been part of Shakti's and Raja's dreams. They had often talked about raising children together. Raja shared Shakti's joy of having a baby, but he was also worried about the expenses of feeding another mouth. As the months passed, Shakti and Raja kept working and trying to save money for the baby's needs. Shakti was very proud of her husband as he worked longer hours to make some extra money to prepare for the baby's arrival.

Raja stayed by her side the entire time, and soon, it was time to go to the hospital to deliver the baby. Poovai took Shakti to the nearby government hospital, and after a short but intense labor pain, her daughter Ponni was born. Since the delivery was normal and there were no complications, Shakti and her baby daughter returned to the temple vicinity after two days in the hospital. Her friends visited the new parents and the baby, complimenting the baby's looks.

To rejoice the birth of Ponni, Poovai distributed sweets to her friends near the temple.

Shakti and Raja enjoyed the new addition to their family and spent countless hours playing with their baby daughter. Both continued to work, and life remained busy. The proud parents forgot their tiredness whenever they saw Ponni's smile. Their faces lit up whenever they saw their daughter sleeping in bliss. Every time they saw their daughter playing without a care in the world, they renewed their resolve to provide the best they could for her. Shakti found work close to where she lived near the temple, making it possible for her to keep her baby daughter beside her while she worked. When she had to go to the neighboring houses to clean and mop, her friends Meena and Nirmala took turns watching her baby. She, in turn, watched their infant children when they went to work. The ever-ready Poovai always lent a helping hand.

Time went by quickly; before she knew it, Ponni was three years old. Her laughter filled the air, making life more bearable for her parents. Shakti was so preoccupied with her work and daughter that she failed to notice that Raja was returning from work later than usual and bringing home less money than normal. She never paid serious attention until she smelled alcohol on his breath.

Shakti confronted Raja, and he admitted that his new friends had persuaded him to stop at a restaurant on his way back from work, where they served alcoholic drinks. The first of many arguments ensued, and Shakti hoped that he would get out of this new habit. But it was not so. Raja kept on making his stops on his way back from work, and she could not do anything to stop him. Raja became louder and more verbally abusive, so Shakti stopped confronting him.

Slowly, days turned into months. Raja started contributing less and less money as he started drinking more and more. Many days, Raja would come back late at night. Initially, Shakti waited to have dinner with him, but Raja told her that he had already eaten. He would go to bed as soon as he returned without spending any time with his daughter or wife. *"At least Raja is coming back to me,"* thought Shakti as she compared herself to some of her homeless friends.

As the days passed, Shakti noticed another change in Raja's behavior toward her. He had always been loving and affectionate with her, but slowly he started avoiding her. At first, she blamed herself, thinking that she was too preoccupied with her daughter and she was not giving enough time to Raja. When one of her friends told her that Raja was seeing another woman, Shakti refused to believe it. Her loving husband would never be unfaithful to her, Shakti thought. When her other friends also told her they had seen Raja with another woman, Shakti's whole world came crashing down. Once again, she confronted Raja and demanded to be told the truth. Surprisingly, Raja confessed immediately; he said he had fallen in love with another woman. He said that initially, he had felt pity toward this other woman because she had recently become a widow, and she had become lonely. But slowly, his feelings for her changed to love.

After confessing to the affair, Raja became even more distant, and their relationship fell apart. There were ugly fights between them. Friends tried to intervene to save Shakti and Raja's marriage, but Raja refused to give up his new love. Slowly, he started staying away during the nights. Initially, it was only once or twice a week, but as time went on, he started staying away for weeks at a time.

Shakti was thus left alone to bring up her daughter. Even though she was overwhelmed with feelings of loneliness and helplessness, she had to be strong for the sake of little Ponni. Shakti put up a brave front and carried on. *Is this why my mother named me Shakti?* she often wondered. Her only consolation was the unconditional love of her daughter. When she saw the trust and love in little Ponni's eyes, Shakti forgot everything else. She hugged her daughter close and rejoiced in the happiness of the moment. "I will do anything for you, little Ponni," she said with tears in her eyes. Her friends comforted her and told her that men can never be trusted. They shared their own experiences of separation and abandonment by the men they had made the mistake of trusting.

After a few months, Shakti slowly adjusted to her new life without Raja. One day, to her immense surprise, he came back. Raja acted as if he had never been away. He brought sweets, toys, and new clothes for his daughter. Shakti's anger melted when she saw the familiar love in his eyes. *He has come back to me!* she thought excitedly. Raja stayed with Shakti and his daughter for a week. She cooked his favorite meals and watched him play with Ponni with a smile on her face.

Everything is going to be fine, she thought happily. But soon, Raja left one morning, saying he was going to work, and that was the last Shakti saw of him for the next three months.

Soon, a new pattern was set. Raja would visit Shakti once every few months and stay with her for a few days. He gave her money for food and bought gifts for her and their daughter. He even took her to her favorite movies. *Just like in old times,* Shakti would think, hoping Raja had come to stay this time. But it was never so. When Raja cuddled up to her in the darkness of the night, Shakti could not stay away. She wanted to feel the comfort of his arms around her once again and the warmth of the love they had once shared.

Much to her dismay, Shakti found out she was pregnant again when Ponni was five. Raja was still playing the role of the 'visiting husband', staying with her for a few days and disappearing again. She had never considered the possibility of another pregnancy. During Raja's next visit, she told him they would have another baby. Instead of the joy she expected, she thought she saw a look of caution on his face. He didn't say much and left after a few days. That was the last time Shakti saw Raja. He stopped visiting her altogether, and she was left alone to fend for herself, her daughter, and soon, her new baby.

The arrival of Kadir, Shakti's son, was an occasion to celebrate. She had prayed for a son, and her heart jumped with joy when she saw his face. She desperately wanted to share her feelings with Raja, but he had stopped visiting her a few months back. She learned from her friends that he had moved in with his new girlfriend. Shakti wiped her tears and focused on her infant son. As always, Poovai helped bring Shakti and her son back from the hospital and cared for Ponni. Soon, Shakti regained her strength and went back to work.

Life was busier than ever. With two young children and no support from her husband, Shakti had to find work every day, either at the flower stall or at the temple, guarding devotees' footwear. She was also a domestic helper in two houses in the neighborhood. Even then, money and food were always scarce. There were days when there was no food, and the children went hungry. Those were the darkest days for Shakti. Her eyes welled up with tears of frustration, hearing her son's cry for food. Again, Poovai came to the rescue. She gave Ponni and Kadir any leftovers she had or bought them food if she had some money. Shakti was immensely grateful for Poovai's help and support.

Living with two young children as a homeless woman, abandoned by her husband, was probably the hardest time in Shakti's life. This was also when she had to become strong and tap into her inner strength, as her name suggested. The joys of motherhood were in sharp contrast to the sorrow of becoming a single mom without any support from her husband. Shakti wiped her tears and moved on, focusing on her children. She had nobody to depend on other than herself.

Chapter 7

A Whistle and a Cane

From early on, the importance of family and marriage in a woman's life was indoctrinated in Shakti's mind by her mother. She was told that according to ancient Hindu ideology, a woman was under the protection of her father and brothers until she got married. After marriage, the responsibility of her care was on her husband. Shakti did not have any reason not to believe this doctrine until she became homeless. Then, her whole world changed, and along with it, her worldview. Suddenly, no father or brothers could help her in her time of need. Her husband, whom she had trusted as a provider and protector, had abandoned her for the sake of another woman. Shakti was left with no choice but to look for alternative support systems.

Shakti had noticed in the first few days of living near the temple that the homeless community she was part of consisted mostly of women and their young children. There were a few older women and a handful of older men. But there were other people who spent a few hours each day near the temple. These were mostly young men in their late teens or their twenties. Initially, Shakti had often wondered who these men were. She soon found out that some of them were adult children of the elderly homeless men and women. They had moved away as they grew older but often visited the temple to see how their parents were doing.

Apart from the visiting family members, the young men who worked in the nearby stores also spent a few hours after work each day near the temple, relaxing with friends. There was an ease of familiarity between the homeless community and these young men. In Shakti's mind, these men were 'local men' in contrast to 'outside men' who were strangers and new to the territory. The local men formed a sort of support system for Shakti and her homeless friends, but they mostly kept to themselves.

Even though her daughter was only eight years old, Shakti had noticed that the teenage daughters of her friends attracted a lot of unwanted attention from the opposite sex, especially the outside men. Shakti had noticed these men making sexual comments among themselves but within the girls' hearing. They never spoke directly with these girls. The girls ignored the outside men and generally kept a distance from them.

The night it happened was etched in Shakti's mind forever because she was constantly on her guard from then on. As usual, the homeless community had settled down for the night. It was about three o'clock in the morning, and Shakti was in a deep slumber. Suddenly, she was rudely awakened by the screams of a girl. Everyone woke up with a start, and the ensuing scene was utter chaos and confusion.

It took Shakti a few minutes to figure out what had happened. An outside man had crept up to snuggle next to a twelve-year-old girl called Vijaya, who was sleeping beside her mother. Vijaya had suddenly woken up to find a stranger's hands on her body, touching her inappropriately. She started screaming, and soon, the whole homeless community was up. A hunt was on to find the stranger, who seemed to have vanished into the darkness.

Some local men who were already near the temple vicinity for an early morning work shift sprang into action. Shakti was immensely grateful to them. They caught the intruder and gave him a sound beating! Followed by multiple warnings of "Never come back!" they let him go. After this intrusive incident, the community of homeless women held an informal meeting the next afternoon. They expressed their fear for their daughters' safety and decided they had to be proactive to prevent such an incident from happening again.

The immediate decision was to let the whole community know that there was an intruder in their midst the previous night. Shakti came up with a proposal. Each woman should keep a whistle with them at nighttime. As soon as they heard the whistle, everyone would know that one of their daughters was in danger, and they could jointly attack the perpetrator. Bagyam, a mother of two young daughters, suggested keeping a sturdy wooden cane to let the intruder know he was not welcome. Everyone agreed, and soon Shakti had her own whistle and cane. Armed with the whistle-cane tool, Shakti slept a little better. But she ensured that her daughter always slept beside her, where she could protect her.

The support system of homeless women like Shakti also included men and women who owned businesses near the temple. The homeless women often bought daily groceries from the store opposite the temple. Most of the time, Shakti had only a few rupees left to buy groceries. Most often, Shakti bought enough groceries for only one meal, which meant that she could buy only one vegetable at a time. Shakti remembered that she often bought one potato, one onion, a tablespoon of salt, a tablespoon of curry powder, and two cups of rice. The storekeeper was kind enough to understand that these homeless women had very limited money, so he catered to their needs and sold them small amounts of groceries they could afford to buy on a given day. Similarly, the nearby restaurant owner also came to the rescue of these women. They did not always have money to buy a complete meal or breakfast, so he would sell small portions of food according to the funds at their disposal. Sometimes, he would give them food on credit, and the women would always repay him later.

Thus, Shakti and her homeless friends wove in and out of challenges and obstacles, always trying to overcome them. In this endeavor, they had to rely not on traditional support systems such as family and marriage but on alternative support systems that included other men and women who were part of the larger community.

Chapter 8

What Did You Call Me?

Living as a homeless woman in a locality where most people lived in homes, Shakti often wondered what they thought of her and the homeless community to which she belonged. She categorized the neighborhood people into two types.

Shakti thought people in the first category were indifferent to her and her friends. They would walk past her as though she were invisible. Such people did not seem to hear the cries of hungry children or the high-pitched voices of elderly women asking for money or food. She called the people in this category 'Zombies'.

Shakti thought that zombie-like people were better than the second category of openly hostile people, which she labeled the 'hostile group'. This group mainly consisted of people who lived in the narrow houses adjacent to the temple compound walls. Their minds were just like their houses, Shakti thought with a smile—*narrow and old!* She knew most people in both categories since they were regular visitors to the temple.

The men and women in the hostile group often commented among themselves as they passed within earshot of Shakti and her friends. A commonly used adjective was 'lazy'. Shakti often heard comments like, "These people are so lazy. They just want free food and money. They don't want to work," or "Look at them! They're always sleeping during the daytime." It looked as if they wanted the homeless people to hear their comments.

Shakti also heard words like 'crazy and mentally ill people', used in reference to the homeless. She wanted to shout back, "I am not crazy; I am just like you on the inside. I am trying to survive by making an honest living. I look different on the outside because my clothes are torn!" Other adjectives that people used to describe the homeless were thieves and beggars. People also blamed the homeless for making the temple compound dirty and accused them of spoiling the temple's image.

When she heard comments like that, Shakti's blood boiled. *If only you knew!* she wanted to scream at these people who were too quick to judge her. She wanted to tell them that she was not born homeless, but circumstances had made her so. She wanted to tell them her story—her happy childhood, dreams and aspirations of coming to Chennai. She wanted to tell them about her struggles—her broken marriage, being a single mom and being homeless. Mainly, she wanted people to understand that she was just like them, and if situations were different, she would have been one of them.

Not all people Shakti encountered near the temple were negative. She found some people, particularly women, who were kind to her. Some were generous in donating money; others donated old clothes. A few people who lived in the neighborhood often gave her leftover food. Some kinder people even wanted to know her story and treated her with respect. They asked her about her family and children. Shakti was thankful that such people existed. They made her day a little more bearable.

Chapter 9

Home Sweet Home

The rain stopped as suddenly as it had started. The sun's rays cast a golden hue on the Earth, and one could spot a dazzling rainbow in the sky. Shakti sat up, suddenly wide awake. She could hear her children playing in the puddle of water nearby. Her face lit up with a smile as she watched her children play. They were her joy and her hope for the future. She leaned back on her makeshift pillow and closed her eyes.

Memories of her past played in her mind like scenes from a movie. Memories of her mother telling her, *"You are my Shakti - my strength."* Shakti thought that her mother would be very proud of her. She wanted to cry out loud to her mom, "I have lived up to my name!" The day Shakti met Raja was a day that changed her life. Her smile broadened as she thought of the happy times they shared. Then, memories of their journey from the village to Chennai brought mixed feelings. The pain of leaving behind her loved ones was mixed with the anticipation of a new life in Chennai with bright prospects for the future. She never forgot the worried look on her parents' faces, along with the love that shone in their eyes.

Suddenly, Shakti's smile was replaced by a frown. The despair of losing her home, the hardships of being homeless, the hunger, the lack of privacy, the loss of Raja's love and support, and the hostile stares of strangers—all hung over her head like dark clouds. When she dwelled on memories of the hardships she had gone through, Shakti's chin went up as if saying, involuntarily, "I will never give up. My mother named me Shakti, after all." She remembered two of her friends who had decided to end their lives, unable to carry on the burden of being single mothers after their husbands had deserted them when their families became homeless. Faced with a similar situation, Shakti had become stronger and focused on her children. She felt proud when she thought of the initial days of despair and hopelessness and how she had survived through it all.

Slowly, her face relaxed, and a small smile crept onto her face. The past was hard without a doubt, she thought, but the future looked promising.

Again, her gaze wandered to her children. Shakti had high hopes for their future. She wanted them to go to school and eventually have access to higher education. She had seen men and women drive to the temple in nice cars, wearing beautiful clothes. Shakti wanted her children to be like them, and she knew that education played a key role in their success. She vowed that she would do everything in her power to help her children become successful in life. Ponni loved going to school and was showing great promise as a top performer, according to her teachers. Kadir, who was only three, was already asking when he could go to school like his sister.

Shakti's biggest dream was to have a small place to call home one day. The very thought of having a small place to cook and stay warm at night in the future made it somehow bearable to live on the streets in the present. Shakti knew that she could not get out of her present situation by herself. All her efforts and energy were spent on daily survival and caring for her children.

With this resolution, Shakti drifted off to sleep, full of happy dreams for the future. She could see a small, cozy home with sunlight streaming in and hear children's laughter as they played.

Shakti's arms closed around herself tightly. Was she holding on to her dream, or keeping herself warm from the cold? Would she indeed wake up one day inside her home? Only time will tell.

Appendix 1

Shakti in Her Own Words

The following section contains excerpts from the informal interviews with Shakti. The interviews were conducted in Tamil (a language spoken in Tamil Nadu). For a full transcript of the interview, contact the author via email provided at the back of the book.

Shakti's happiness and excitement about her wedding:

"On my wedding day, we had invited so many people, relatives from both sides. I wore a new sari and blouse. We had cooked a lot of food, and the guests ate for two days. I remember it so well."

Her joy in receiving gold jewelry from her mother:

"On my wedding day, my mother gave me a pair of gold earrings and a gold necklace. I felt so proud! My friends were so jealous of me."

Shakti's anger and frustration about her husband's infidelity:

"My husband left me for another woman. Her husband died recently, and she is all alone. She is older than me. I think he is doing her a favor. They cannot marry because I am still his wife. She is earning a lot of money, more than me, because she works in a hospital. She also got a lot of money after her husband died. She lives in a rented house. She took my husband."

"In the beginning, I did not believe that he was seeing another woman. People used to come and tell me that they saw him with another woman. I refused to believe. They said that they saw him in the theater with her. Then, one day, he told me that he was going to be with her because she was a widow and she needed someone. Then I said, 'Look, if you want to give her money or any other help, do it, but if you have sexual relations with

*her, my children and I will commit suicide and die.'
He did not listen. I tried to kill myself by jumping
into a lake, but I survived."*

Shakti's feelings about her 'visiting husband':

*"He comes over whenever he wants to. I
feel very bad about that. He usually comes in
the afternoons when the children are playing
or asleep, and he calls me. He wants me to go
with him to this abandoned house to have sex. I
don't want to go, but what can I do? He is very
insistent, and I cannot say no. He usually brings
small gifts like lipstick or other makeup for me.
He even asks me to wear a particular sari or put
on additional makeup. He is very demanding. I
generally end up doing what he wants. I know he
comes to me with one thing on his mind. He sets
the stage from the beginning. He takes me out to
a movie that I have been wanting to see for days.
After that, I feel terrible. I don't want to have sex
with him after he has been with another woman,
but he never listens. I go around feeling bad for
a long time."*

On the breakup of her marriage:

"He is a man; he can do whatever he wants. My greatest fear was that he would leave me. Even if he was a drunkard and he beat me up, it was still OK. At least he was with me. Now, he's with another woman; is it not wrong?"

On the sexual activities under cover of darkness:

"Of course, everybody knows that those two are having sex. We all know it. Sometimes, the noises they make! It is disgusting, you know. We won't take notice of it, but what about the children? You know everybody sleeps in the open, and what would the children learn if they saw such a thing? I think those types of women are really shameless. Why can't they take themselves and their lovers to some isolated place instead of doing it in a place where children are around?"

On feeling helpless about not being able to provide food for her children:

"My children are very young and cry for food all the time. What can I do? I don't have money to buy food for them all the time. Some days *are especially bad. I don't get any food from my employer and there is no money. Then, the children start crying and ask for food, especially if they see other children eating. They don't understand that I'm trying to put any food in their stomach. They keep asking for this and that, and I really get mad and shout at them. If the children are really hungry, then I go begging for food."*

On her fears for the safety of her daughter:

"Women with young daughters are constantly afraid of men and what they could do to their daughters. If we had a home, things would be different, but we are homeless, and here, we are constantly exposed to dangers from men who tease women for fun. Near the temple, it is worse. When we are sitting there, men who are just walking past make obscene comments and jokes. The men from the slum near the beach are the worst; they come and sleep next to our daughters in the middle of the night. It is so dark that you don't even know who it is. We have to constantly check to see that nobody is sleeping next to our daughters. That is when we feel the absence of homes."

On borrowing money:

"One time, my son suddenly became ill when he was very young. I took him to the hospital, and they said that he needed twelve injections. So I had to borrow money to get him treated. I still have not repaid the money."

On living near the temple:

"We came to stay here for the night, and we continued staying here. We got to know the people and continue to stay here. Where else can I go with the kids? Where else can they sleep safely? It is so scary to sleep outside these days. That is why we stay close to the temple."

On the hazards of being homeless:

"Life is very hard. First of all, we have to worry about the weather. If there is wind or heavy rain, we do not have a place to sleep. For example, last night it rained. I gathered my kids near me, and we all sat there waiting for the rain to stop. Only after the rain stopped did we all get up and remove the excess water from the floor. Then I dried the floor *and made my children sleep on old saris. I did not want to go to anybody's house."*

On 'outside men':

"The men who bother us and our daughters are not men who are known to us. Our men do not harass us. It is only strangers who do this. In fact, our men protect us from outside men."

On creating networks with other homeless women:

"We women also arm ourselves with whatever is ready, like old shoes, wooden sticks, and whistles. We keep them close to us when we sleep. If one woman wakes up instantly, everybody's awake. We are like a pack of crows. If a stranger is seen near the temple and appears suspicious, somebody gives out a warning signal, usually a whistle, and everyone gathers in one place. Because I am with other people, we could just manage. We sleep huddled together in a corner and watch out for each other all the time."

Appendix 2

Life Sketches of Five Homeless Women

The following section contains life sketches of five homeless women, presented in order of age from youngest to oldest. Their stories about their early life, migration to major cities in search of a better future, seeking employment as daily wagers, marriage, and family life, their separation from their husbands, becoming single mothers, facing harassment and humiliation from the institutions of the larger society, growing old, and dealing with feelings of loneliness and despair all resonate with incidents in Shakti's life.

Malar

Malar's parents had originally migrated to Chennai from a nearby village before her birth. She was the youngest of two sisters and a brother. Her mother was a domestic helper, and her father worked as a temple watchman. They could live in a room owned by the temple and pay rent to the temple authorities because he was a temple employee.

When Malar reached puberty, her father and brother started searching for a suitable marriage partner for her. Her mother had died by then, and her sister was married. Malar's father and brother first decided upon Rajendran, a homeless youth who lived near the temple along with his family. Soon, word spread among their friends and relatives that Malar and Rajendran were getting married. But then, her father decided that Rajendran was not a suitable match for his daughter because he was homeless. Malar, however, felt that she had to marry Rajendran. She liked him and his family and was afraid of public ridicule.

When she told her father and brother that she would marry only Rajendran, they started abusing her physically. She ran away from home and went to live with Rajendran's mother, who not only took her in but also married her to Rajendran. Thus, Malar started her married life as a homeless woman. Soon she had two children and began to work as a domestic helper in the houses near the temple. Her husband worked as a daily wage laborer or electrician's helper.

Soon after Malar had her third child, her husband started having an affair with another woman. Malar initially refused to believe this when people told her about it until she finally saw her husband and the other woman together. She tried everything to save her marriage. She cried and begged him to leave the other woman; she threatened and tried to commit suicide. Despite all this, Rajendran left Malar and moved in with the other woman. She did not know why he broke up with her but wondered if it was because the other woman was rich and lived in a rented apartment.

Even though Malar and her husband no longer lived together, he visited her whenever he liked and spent a day or two with her. Sometimes, he helped her financially but expected sexual intimacy from her during his visits. She never went to her husband's house but sometimes sent her children to him when she needed money urgently. She was very unhappy about her relationship with her husband and constantly worried about her future and her children.

Malar worked in two houses as a domestic helper. She also worked as a janitor in a doctor's office. With the money she made from these jobs, Malar looked after her three children. She sent the eldest two to a nearby school. The doctor she worked with provided free medicines for Malar and her children. She was worried that she might be pregnant with her fourth child. She was scared to have an abortion and did not know what to do. Malar hoped that one day, her husband would realize his mistake and come back to her. In the meantime, she tolerated his drunkenness. She hoped that one day, her children would get a good education and live in an apartment.

Gangabai

Gangabai was a tall woman in her forties. A good narrator, she talked about her life from her childhood, and when she narrated the recent tragedy in her family, her eyes filled with tears. She was married to a much older man her parents chose when she was twelve. They had three children. When the youngest child was a year old, Gangabai fell in love with a married neighbor and had an affair with him. Once, she gave all her gold jewels to her lover because he was having financial problems. Her parents and her husband came to know of the affair, and there were fights, particularly with her husband. Gangabai tried to commit suicide by hanging herself but survived.

After a while, Gangabai's lover wanted to leave their village and move to Chennai. In the meantime, his wife had died. Gangabai decided to elope with him. She took her youngest daughter with her. They lived in different locations in Chennai and tried to make a living. Gangabai and her lover tried out various jobs to make ends meet. They set up a small store in a slum, but people in the slum started to buy things on credit and never paid. Then, they tried mobile food vending for a couple of years, but that did not bring any profit either. Gangabai sold all her gold jewels one by one and eventually reached a stage where they could not pay rent. In the meantime, Gangabai had four more children, and the family became poorer and poorer.

The landlord threw Gangabai and her family out when the rent became overdue, so the whole family became homeless. They went to the temple to stay there temporarily but ended up staying permanently. She worked as a domestic helper in two houses and her lover worked as an ice-cream vendor. Her eldest daughter works in a movie theater, her twelve-year-old son works in a store, and the youngest daughter helps Gangabai with domestic work.

Life near the temple was very hard for Gangabai. There was no place to sleep, especially when it rained. The money that she earned as a domestic help was not enough to feed her family, and her lover worked only part-time because of his advanced age and health problems. She supplemented her income by begging. She was quick to notice foreign tourists who visited the temple; they usually gave more money than local tourists.

Gangabai's days followed a routine. She slept near the temple when everyone had settled down. In the early morning hours, she bathed near the water pump, which was located on the roadside near the temple for public use. She bathed in cold water while it was still dark to escape being stared at. Then, she went to work as a domestic helper in her employer's house. At noon, she returned, bringing leftover food given by her employer. She supplemented this by buying food from the restaurant opposite the temple if she had enough money or, more cheaply, from the food vendor.

Afternoons were spent either napping or talking with friends near the temple. Sometimes, she found extra work making fresh flower garlands near the temple. During evenings, she and her children occasionally went to movies or else watched television at her employer's house. Dinner again depended on how much money they had that day at their disposal. Around eleven at night, after everybody had settled down, Gangabai found a good spot to spread her mat for the night. The whole family slept huddled together either on old saris or coir mats spread on the ground. Gangabai preferred to sleep next to her daughter because she was worried about her daughter's safety during nights when strangers were more likely to bother her.

Gangabai thought that Chennai was the worst place on Earth and that life in her village was much better. She talked about her home and family in the village and wanted to return. But she felt that she had betrayed her husband by eloping and that people in her village, including her husband, would never forgive her for that. She would rather die in Chennai than go back to face her family and friends.

Kamala

Kamala, a widow in her fifties, was proud of her involvement in a political party. She was disabled; when she walked, she limped, and walking was slow and painful. Kamala's parents migrated to Chennai when she was young. Her father worked as an agricultural laborer, and her mother sold flowers. Kamala's father died when she was seven years old, and when she was seventeen, her mother arranged her marriage. Her husband was an alcoholic and abused Kamala throughout their married life of thirty-five years. They had two daughters and earned their livelihood by maintaining a small store in the area where they lived. They sold everyday essentials like cigarettes, cookies, soda, and soap.

Kamala did not talk about what her life was like when she was married except to say that she and her husband, along with their children, lived in a rented room for a number of years. She also mentioned that a few years before his death, her husband left her and their children for another woman.

After her husband's death, Kamala tried to manage the store alone, but eventually, she had to close it. After that, there was no money to pay rent, and slowly her deposit money ran out, and the landlord threw her out. Initially, Kamala did not know where to go. Somebody mentioned the temple to her, and she decided to spend a few days there. Five years later, it had become her home.

Kamala's daughters, who were married, visited her only rarely, and most of the time she was alone near the temple. Because of her handicap, any kind of physical activity was hard for her. She sold fresh flowers to tourists near the temple, which was her primary income source. She had to source flowers from a far-away market that required her to travel by bus. However, the buses were always crowded, and Kamala found it very hard to get in and out of buses due to her weak leg. So she avoided going to the market and asked a friend to bring the flowers for her from the market. To supplement the income from selling flowers, Kamala takes recourse to begging. People were more sympathetic toward her due to her handicap.

Valli

Born and brought up in Chennai, Valli was a widow, and her life story was one in which alcohol and abuse played major roles. She did not know her exact age, but she guessed she might be in her late sixties. She claimed that she had lived near the temple the longest and that most of the other homeless women came to the temple long after she and her family did.

Valli and her husband had six children, and she lived in a rented house when he was alive. Her husband, an alcoholic, gradually lost his health, becoming too ill to work. He went from hospital to hospital in search of treatment for alcoholism. One day, the family could not afford to pay rent any longer, so the landlord threw them out. Thereafter, Valli and her husband moved to the temple with their four unmarried children. Two of her daughters were already married and had moved away.

Valli and her husband had heard about the temple and had visited it a number of times, occasionally spending a night or two near the temple before returning to their place. When Valli's family became homeless, she thought of a homeless woman with whom she had made friends near the temple. The friend advised Valli that the temple vicinity was safe, especially for small children. So Valli's family moved to the temple with the intention of staying only temporarily. However, soon after they moved near the temple,

Valli's husband's health deteriorated, and he eventually died despite many hospital visits. Valli continued to live near the temple and started working as a domestic help in three or four houses to support her children. Two of Valli's adult sons were alcoholics with no steady jobs. Instead of helping their mother, they demanded money from her. When Valli refused to give them money, they beat her up. Valli had gone to the police station a number of times to report the abuse, but her sons continued to harass her. Two of Valli's daughters married early and suffered from bad marriages. They eventually returned to live with their mother near the temple and work as domestic helps in nearby houses.

Valli worked in two houses as a domestic help and made about three to five hundred rupees per month. With this money, she had to meet all her expenses. Her health was not as it used to be, and she suffered more from her weak leg. Despite all her problems, Valli was a very proud woman who refused to beg for food or clothing. She claimed to have lived near the temple the longest, for more than twenty years.

Rajam

Rajam was in her late seventies. She was one of the ten basket weavers who migrated from Salem to Chennai in search of a better life. She lived with her son, who was in his late twenties, on a small street next to the temple. Their belongings were all stacked in a corner on the roadside, and they slept on the concrete pavement adjacent to the road. They did not have any blankets or other bedding, and they were very poor. Rajam, like many other homeless women, had known better times in her younger days when she lived in her village. She lived with her husband in their own house. When the demand for bamboo baskets decreased, they migrated to Chennai. They sold their home and belongings and moved to Chennai in search of a broader market for bamboo baskets.

In Chennai, Rajam and her husband lived as homeless people in different locations over the years before moving to live near the temple. Rajam always referred to her husband as her 'old man' (kilavan) and spoke about him with love and affection. She spoke of how kind and considerate he was. He followed her wherever she went and cooked for her. When she spoke of her life with him, tears gathered in her eyes and she had to pause before continuing.

However, Rajam's old man also lived with two other women at the same time. She swore that even though he had five children from each woman, he loved only her. She claimed that the only reason he lived with the other women was that she did not give birth to a much-desired son. So he asked her permission to bring the other women into the household (the second wife also produced five daughters).

After her husband's death, Rajam's life took a turn for the worse, and her economic situation deteriorated. Eventually, the children of her husband's mistresses threw her out of their house, where they had all lived for so many years. She moved to live near the temple with her youngest son (he was born after her husband had taken the two women as mistresses). Rajam's son was physically and mentally handicapped and was dependent on Rajam for his survival. She brought food to him every day, and if she did not feed him in time, he got angry and fought with her.

Rajam said she and her family had never done any work other than basket weaving. Even though her eyesight is failing, she still makes and sells baskets. However, the income from selling bamboo baskets was not enough to meet their needs, so she supplemented her income by begging.

Rajam's greatest concern was her son. She worried about him constantly and about his future. Her greatest ambition was to see him married. Then, she says, she can die peacefully, knowing that she kept her promise to her dying husband that she would never abandon their son. Rajam has a granddaughter with whom she wants to arrange her son's marriage, but the girl's father is totally against the match. Rajam hoped that he would soon change his mind.

Epilogue

Great strides have been taken by the Indian government in recent years to provide financial assistance, free transportation, and low-cost housing to women living below the poverty line. Free or low-cost shelters and hostels are available to improve the lives of migrant and working women. Many NGOs offer interest-free loans and free training to women who want to start their small businesses.

Preliminary follow-up data collected in recent months offer an interesting insight into the present conditions of homeless women like Shakti. Many major temples in Chennai have erected compound walls to discourage unwanted visitors. Hence, the homeless have to find alternative places to escape the hot and humid climate of Chennai. The newly built metro railway stations in different parts of the city seem to have unwittingly come to the rescue of the homeless, particularly the elderly. Many women who spent the entire day in front of the temple a few years earlier said they spent the hot afternoons in the shade of the covered railway station near the temple, where huge ceiling fans blew hot air, bringing some comfort.

Many homeless women seen near the temple said that they stayed there till lunchtime because, during that time, they were given free food by the temple visitors or the temple staff. Some women, especially the elderly, were engaged in soliciting devotees and tourists for money. This activity was not encouraged by the temple staff, who accused these women of using the money to buy alcohol and engaging in unruly behavior near the temple. Devotees and tourists complained that they were not able to enjoy their visit to the temple. Such women were classified as 'beggars'.

A few younger women who presented a professional appearance were employed by the store owners to make fresh flower garlands, depending on the demand for garlands and the supply of fresh flowers. Many elderly women expressed concern about not receiving the financial aid given by the government because they did not have an address or identity card. Some mentioned they were eligible to get the monthly stipend, but their registration cards were back in their village, or their children threw them out of their home and took away their identity cards.

What happened to Shakti, her family, and her friends? Despite multiple attempts to locate her, Shakti could not be found near the temples or other places where she spent much of her time with her family and friends only a few years ago. Did her dream of living in a home come true? Did her children stay in school? Did she and her friends have access to the opportunities available through government grants and other programs? Have most homeless families living near the temples been relocated to other areas like railway stations and bus terminals? Has the traditional role of temples in supporting the homeless community changed over time?

While providing some answers, this project raised some more important questions mentioned above that could only be answered by future research. I hope that through the story of Shakti, I have added value to my readers' understanding of the challenges faced by the homeless women of Chennai and the tenacity and inner strength with which they overcome these challenges.

Photo Gallery

These photographs were taken in 2024 as part of a preliminary follow-up study. They show both continuity and change in the lives of homeless people living in Chennai (see epilogue).

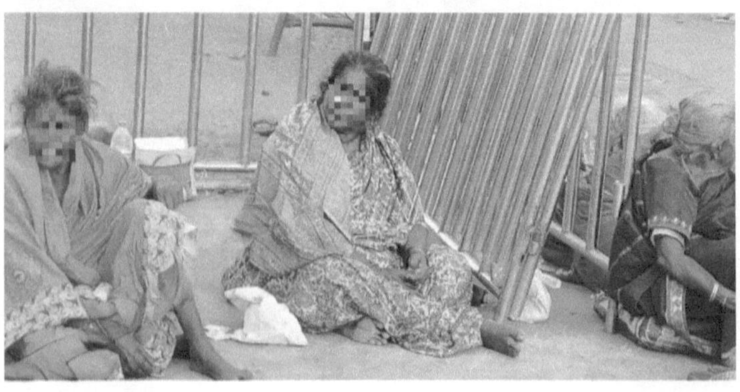

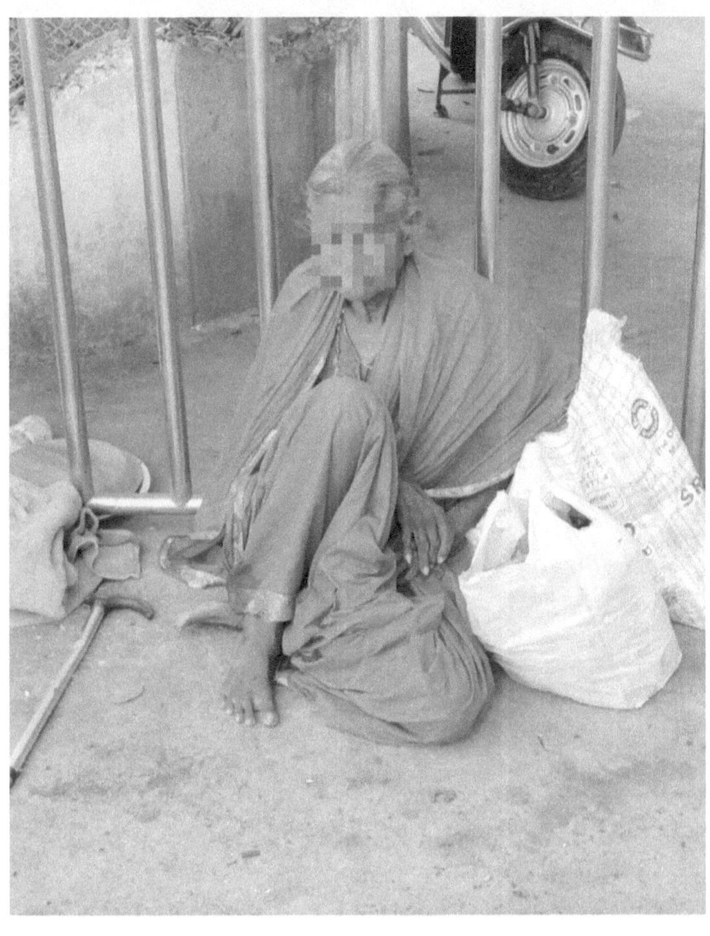